Hundred Years of Happiness

Written by
Thanhhà Lại

Illustrated by
Nguyên Quang and Kim Liên

HARPER
An Imprint of HarperCollinsPublishers

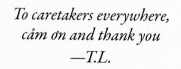

To caretakers everywhere,
cảm ơn and thank you
—T.L.

For our grandmothers
—N.Q. and K.L.

Hundred Years of Happiness
Text copyright © 2022 by Thanhhà Lại
Illustrations copyright © 2022 by Phung Nguyên Quang and Huynh Thi Kim Liên
All rights reserved. Manufactured in Italy.
No part of this book may be used or reproduced in any manner whatsoever without written permission except
in the case of brief quotations embodied in critical articles and reviews. For information address HarperCollins
Children's Books, a division of HarperCollins Publishers, 195 Broadway, New York, NY 10007.
www.harpercollinschildrens.com

Library of Congress Control Number: 2020949341
ISBN 978-0-06-302692-6

The artist used Photoshop to create the illustrations for this book.
Typography by Dana Fritts
21 22 23 24 25 RTLO 10 9 8 7 6 5 4 3 2 1
❖
First Edition

E very day after school An greets her grandparents in Vietnamese. She massages Bà's hands and rubs her back. She sings a song Bà once taught her about a baby elephant. An swings one arm in front of her face. Bà suddenly swings a pretend trunk too.

But as Bà eats the day's soft treat, a blankness claims her expression and a thin smoke clouds her eyes. She doesn't remember the fruit is persimmon. At times Bà forgets who An is. But she never forgets Ông. The two of them are always next to each other, breaths swirling into one.

An knows not to ask Ông if the gấc seeds they are waiting for have arrived. But today Ông beams as he shows off huge seeds, black and wrinkly. "Finally we can make Bà's favorite dish from our wedding, many floating years ago."

Ông says, "She smiled at me and I knew all my days
I would sweat and plan to confirm our relatives' wish,
'Trăm năm hạnh phúc,' *hundred years of happiness.*"

Ông has tried to untangle Bà's memories with many foods, many photographs, and many stories. As childhood friends, he and Bà had crafted turtles from gấc seeds, resembling shells, and now he hopes the seeds will help her remember.

Bà reaches for a seed and massages it among her fingers. An hints, "Turtle?" But Bà returns the seed to Ông's palm.

For days the seeds soak in warm water. Finally tiny
white sprouts burst through tight mouths. Everyone,
including Bà, claps when Ông declares the seeds are
ready to be cocooned inside fluffy soil.

More weeks pass before fragile tendrils climb the air. Ông hums.

An asks Bà, "Guess our surprise?"

Bà clutches An's hand. "Little Tâm, the sweet potato shoots are ready for planting."

The question and answer mismatch. Still, everyone is delighted Bà has remembered her sister and a distant world.

Four vines wilt as if deflated in spirit. "Sixteen are plenty," Ông reasons. If he is worried, An cannot tell. She pats the back of his hand, the way Bà used to comfort her.

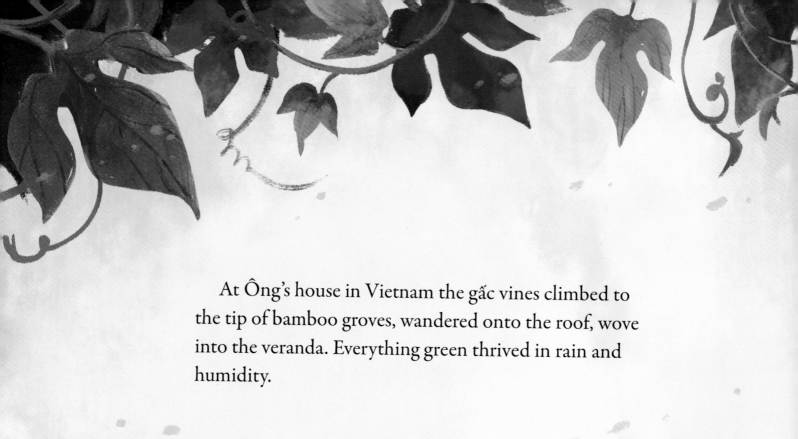

At Ông's house in Vietnam the gấc vines climbed to the tip of bamboo groves, wandered onto the roof, wove into the veranda. Everything green thrived in rain and humidity.

An tells Bà, "Ông says you touched any plant and it grew. You're magic." Bà doesn't react, though she lets An hold her wrist and together they flick magic onto each vine.

When the gấc flowers bloom, the whole house awakens
early to witness An and Ông breaking off the males to
pollinate the females.

Dad says, "An is a busy bee."

Mom laughs.

Bà stares at the flowers as she sips tea.

Days later An squeals, counting eight green babies, fat and round as marbles. Ông hushes her and warns the bashful fruits will drop from too much attention.

After long months, six fruits mature into globes dangling like
cooled tiny suns. An chooses the one ripening to deepest orange.
Its prickly skin stabs as if covered in miniature puppies' teeth.

Ông slices a sun, exposing crimson gooey pockets protecting the seeds. Then An and Ông smoosh the fruit's red flesh against glutinous rice, adding a dash of sugar and sprinkles of coconut milk.

Bà surprises them and joins in. They laugh at each other's dyed palms.

Somehow crimson hands make them feel better when the first batch burns.

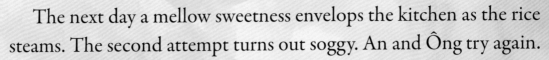

The next day a mellow sweetness envelops the kitchen as the rice steams. The second attempt turns out soggy. An and Ông try again. As red lines ink under their fingernails, the grains in the third batch plump and soften perfectly. They call everyone to have a taste.

Bà's nose wrinkles and her lips quiver as she leans close to the mound of xôi gấc. Filaments of yellow fleck orange grains.

Bà accepts a spoonful. So does An. So do her parents.

A fatty, nutty, clean, chewy sweetness, fragranted by drifts of a flower.

Bà tilts her face and blinks as if bothered by the smoke in her eyes.

An reaches toward Ông's hand, ready to offer comfort.

Bà savors another bite.
A deep inhale, nostrils inflating as if ready to fly.
Then the smoke fades and Bà's eyes dance. Her lips curve
into a crescent moon. Cheekbones inflate into boiled eggs. She
whispers, "Trăm năm hạnh phúc, *hundred years of happiness*."

Ông blinks moisture.

An feels as if a firecracker might flare out her mouth and explode.

By the last bite, smoke has reclaimed Bà's eyes, and blankness her expression.

"That's it?" An blurts, disappointment erasing the nutty sweetness on her tongue.

Ông's cheekbones lift toward the sky as he answers, "Let's soak twenty more seeds."

A Note from the Author

In 1994, I visited Vietnam for the first time after fleeing as a child refugee almost two decades earlier. I went to an open market with my mom and saw shoppers bargaining for orange-red fruit. As I held one, amused by its prickly skin, my mom said I would finally know what authentic xôi gấc tasted like. I had eaten xôi gấc made by dyeing white grains red. But the real thing, oh my, had gold filaments interwoven into the glutinous rice. And the taste, a nutty sweetness enhanced by a soft fragrance. I brought back three seeds. Recently I found them shriveled in my jewelry box. Visions of turtle shells, wedding tradition, aging couple, greenhouse in Southern California. And so . . .

A Gấc Sticky Rice Recipe
(based on a recipe from illustrator Kim Liên's mom)

ADULT SUPERVISION REQUIRED—ASK A GROWN-UP FOR HELP.

4 cups sticky rice

1-2 gấc fruits (fully ripened)

1 cup coconut milk

1 tablespoon rice wine

1 tablespoon vegetable oil

1 teaspoon salt

1 cup sugar

shredded coconut (optional)

1. Rinse and drain the sticky rice twice to clean the rice.

2. Soak the rice in water overnight. Add the salt.

3. Rinse again and let it drain in a strainer.

4. Cut the gấc fruit in half; use a spoon to take out the red seeds.

5. Put the seeds in a bowl and pour in the rice wine. Use your hands to strip the red arils off the dark seeds. Set the dark seeds to the side, then stir and form a red paste.

6. Mix the drained rice and red gấc paste thoroughly. Let sit for 30 minutes.

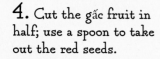

7. Add the vegetable oil and mix gently.

8. Steam at medium heat for 20 to 30 minutes until the rice turns soft, round, and shiny.

9. In the meantime, mix the coconut milk and sugar.

10. Pour 1/3 of the coconut milk-sugar mixture over the rice, stir gently, and cover. Cook for 10 minutes, then repeat, adding 1/3 of the mixture each time until you've used all the coconut milk-sugar mixture.

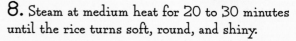

11. Put the dark seeds on top of the rice (for decoration only). Serve with shredded coconut if desired.